This book belongs to

_____

# A Real Little Bunny

————— *A Sequel to* —————

## The Velveteen Rabbit

**Jennifer Greenway**

*Illustrated By*
**Robyn Officer**

ARIEL BOOKS

Library of Congress Cataloging-in-Publication Data

Greenway, Jennifer.
A real little bunny / by Jennifer Greenway.
p. cm.
"A sequel to The velveteen rabbit by Margery Williams."
"Ariel books."
Summary: After he becomes Real and goes to live with the other wild rabbits in the
woods, the velveteen rabbit returns to visit the boy who used to own him and meets the
new toy rabbit that has taken his place.

ISBN 0-8362-4936-4 : $14.95
[1. Rabbits—Fiction.    2. Toys—Fiction.]      I. Title.
PZ7.G8525Re   1993
[Fic]—dc20               92–37149
CIP
AC

# $\mathcal{A}$
# $\mathcal{R}eal\ \mathcal{L}ittle\ \mathcal{B}unny$

—— *A Sequel to* ——
## THE VELVETEEN RABBIT

Once there was a toy rabbit who became REAL. His story is told in a book called *The Velveteen Rabbit*. At first the little Velveteen Rabbit was Real only to the Boy who loved him. As is the case with most toys, this happened after the Boy had played with the Velveteen Rabbit so much that most of his fur was loved off and his once-bright button eyes were faded and scratched. The Velveteen Rabbit loved the Boy back and never imagined he would ever have to leave him. But one day the Boy became sick with scarlet fever, and when he was well again, the doctor told his nanny to get rid of the Velveteen Rabbit. "That toy's a mass of germs!" the doctor said. "Burn it at once!" And so the little Velveteen Rabbit was tossed out on the rubbish heap with the bed quilt and the rest of the toys the Boy had played with while he was sick.

Then the nursery magic Fairy (the fairy who takes care of all the toys children have truly loved) came and turned the Velveteen Rabbit into an honest-to-goodness live Little Rabbit and took him to live with the wild rabbits. Now, instead of worn velveteen, the Little Rabbit had soft, shiny fur. Instead of buttons, he now had velvety black eyes that sparkled when he was happy and grew cloudy when he was sad. And instead of being stuffed with sawdust, he had real hind legs, and, for the first time, he could hop about wherever he chose in the Big Wide World.

Of course, being Real and living in the forest was very different from being a toy in the nursery. There was much that was new and delightful to the Little Rabbit. It was wonderful to wiggle his ears and nose without the mainsprings and keys that the mechanical toys had to depend on to move. It was even more wonderful to hop around the roots of the tall, mossy trees, or turn somersaults whenever he felt like it. And what a joy it was to smell the fresh green grass and nibble on stalks of sweet clover, things he had certainly never been able to do when he was just a toy and lived inside a big wooden cupboard in the nursery.

Nevertheless, the Little Rabbit could not help feeling a bit strange in his new home. The other wild rabbits were nice enough, but they could not understand why he knew so little about living in the wild. "Do you mean to say you've never dug a

carrot in a farmer's garden before?" they would sniff. "Or pulled up a dandelion root? What a strange creature you are!"

When the older rabbits told stories of running away from foxes and hunters, the Little Rabbit always asked too many questions. "What does a fox look like?" he asked one night, for there had been no toy foxes in the nursery.

This made the other young rabbits feel quite superior, for at least they knew how to recognize a fox hole and how to spot a hunter's cap across a field. "Didn't your mother teach you anything when you were growing up?" they asked. The Little Rabbit felt very awkward then, for of course he did not have a mother, and he'd done all his growing up in the Boy's nursery.

But one evening at supper, which is when the wild rabbits tell their stories, the Little Rabbit tried to tell them about his old life in the nursery. He spoke of his friend the Skin Horse. The Skin Horse was the oldest toy in the nursery, he explained. It was the Skin Horse who first told the Velveteen Rabbit what it was to be Real.

At first the wild rabbits were curious, for they had never heard of a Skin Horse. They asked him many questions. But when they found out the Skin Horse was stuffed with sawdust and could not gallop and jump over fences as real horses did, they quickly lost interest. "Tell us something exciting!" they said.

So the Little Rabbit told them of the wonderful games he and the Boy had played in the garden, like pretending to be sailors on a sailboat or explorers in the jungle. But the other rabbits only turned up their tails at his stories. "What nonsense!" they declared. They dared not admit that they had never seen a sailboat and that they did not even know what a jungle was.

"Why would anyone even want to sail on a boat?" they asked. "It sounds most uncomfortable!"

Even when the Little Rabbit told them how once he had almost gone to the seashore, the wild rabbits were not impressed. "How awful all that sand must be!" they cried. "And all those waves splashing about everywhere! We would much rather stay here in the forest!"

After that, the Little Rabbit never spoke about his old life. Instead, he did his best to learn to be a proper wild rabbit. But every so often a queer melancholy feeling came over him, and he hopped off all by himself to the edge of the forest. There he stared out over the fields at the house where he had once lived with the Boy. He longed to go there and see again the garden with the raspberry thicket where he had played so happily, and visit his friend the Skin Horse. Most of all, he longed to see the Boy who had made him Real.

But the field was big and wide. Sometimes the farmers let their dogs run wild there, and the Little Rabbit was afraid to leave the safety of the forest.

Autumn passed, and then winter. Slowly, the Little Rabbit learned all the things the other wild rabbits knew. He learned that foxes had red fur, thick bushy tails, long pointy noses, and sharp teeth. He learned that hunters often wore red, and how to run fast to get out of their way. He learned how to dig up potatoes and carrots from the farmers' gardens, and where to find dandelions and sweet clover. And as he learned the ways of the wild, the other rabbits no longer made fun of him. And by and by the Little Rabbit began to think less about his old home.

Spring came, and the world again grew bright. The sun warmed the air, and every day the sky was a brilliant blue. In the fields the smell of blooming violets and tender new grass filled the air. Lettuce, carrots, and peas began to grow in the farmers' gardens, and all the wild rabbits were happy at having plenty to eat.

One lovely warm day the Little Rabbit was playing chase-your-tail with a big brown rabbit named Chestnut. The two friends had been going at it all morning and were quite tired out. They'd just stretched out in the shade of a big oak tree to take a nap when they heard footsteps coming toward them. Chestnut instantly ran off and hid under a wild mulberry bush. But the Little Rabbit was frozen to the spot, for there was something familiar-sounding about the footsteps. So he stared straight ahead, his nose twitching expectantly.

A moment later three boys came running through the bracken, laughing and calling out to one another. "That sounds like His voice," the Little Rabbit thought, almost afraid to look. Sure enough, in the center of the three was the Boy himself!

The Little Rabbit's heart suddenly felt so big and light he could hardly hold it inside him. He hopped forward, until he was right in front of the three boys, then he kept very still and waited for the Boy to recognize him.

"Look!" cried one of the other boys. "There's a rabbit!" And he stamped his foot and raised his hand as if he were trying to scare the Little Rabbit away.

"Leave him alone!" cried the Boy, staring at the Little Rabbit thoughtfully. "He looks just like my old velveteen Bunny that was lost when I had scarlet fever."

When the Little Rabbit heard that, he felt so happy he could hardly bear it. But one of the Boy's friends said, "Don't be silly! I know, let's be hunters and shoot at him."

And both the other boys raised up their hands like guns and came charging right at him!

The Little Rabbit was so frightened he trembled all over, even his little tail. But he would not move, for he so wanted the Boy to know that it was really him.

The first boy looked down disgustedly. "I don't know what's the matter with that rabbit," he said. "He's no good for chasing or anything!" He turned to the others. "Come along! Let's have a race!" Whooping and hollering, the two strange boys ran off toward the open fields, but the Boy lingered behind and gazed at the Little Rabbit with an odd expression.

"He really does look like my old Bunny," he murmured to himself. "Even his eyes have the exact same look." When the Little Rabbit heard that, he almost somersaulted for joy. But just as he was about to hop closer, the Boy turned around and shouted, "Hey! Wait for me!" and ran off after the other boys, leaving the Little Rabbit all alone.

As soon as the boys had disappeared, Chestnut hopped over. He was shocked at the Little Rabbit's behavior. "What's wrong with you?" he demanded. "Why didn't you run away?" But the Little Rabbit said nothing, for all he could think about was seeing the Boy again. Right then, he decided that he would wait until after dark when the farmers had called their dogs in from the fields, and then he would go to the Boy's house. Surely then the Boy would know that he was really his very own toy Bunny that had been lost!

Perhaps the Boy would even pick him up and whisper a story in his ear, the Little Rabbit thought, a wonderful story about a bright blue sailing ship that would carry them across the sea to a jungle full of strange flowers and trees and fierce lions and striped tigers. Or perhaps they would play a game together in the raspberry thicket. Now that the Little Rabbit was Real, they could have much better games than before. Why, he and the Boy could chase each other and play hide 'n' seek and captain of the castle or whatever else they chose. Just thinking about it made the Little Rabbit feel warm and happy inside.

The Little Rabbit was careful to say nothing of his plan to the other rabbits. That night he waited until they had all eaten their supper and were nodding off to sleep under the stars, then he slipped away and set out across the fields.

When he reached the house, it was all lit up, and the Boy and his family were just finishing their dinner. Luckily, the low windows in the living room had been left open a crack, so the Little Rabbit had only to hop inside.

The house seemed very big and strange to him after so much time in the forest. Tall glass-paned cabinets gleamed from the corners of the room. The polished wood floors were so smooth that he kept slipping on them. And the lamps shone so brightly that they dazzled him, and for a moment he could not remember how to get to the Boy's room.

At last, he came to the big staircase. He could hear voices nearby, and he felt very afraid. But he bravely started up, even though it was hard. The stairs seemed very tall, for of course he had never climbed them himself before.

When he finally reached the top, he saw the door to the nursery at once. It was open, and the light was out. His heart beating faster and faster, he crept in.

Everything in the quiet room was just as he remembered it. In one corner stood the big yellow wooden cupboard where all the toys were kept. In front of it was the old rag rug, faded from years of small feet walking across it. And against the wall was the Boy's bed where the Little Rabbit had nestled so cozily all those nights long ago. A crescent moon shone through the window, giving everything a silvery glow. The Little Rabbit thought of how he used to look at that very moon as he lay beside the sleeping Boy, and he felt as if he had come home at last.

Suddenly he spotted his old friend the Skin Horse standing in a far corner.

"Hello!" he cried excitedly. "It's me! I've been living in the forest and now I've come home."

But the Skin Horse didn't move or say anything, even when the Little Rabbit nudged him with his paw. "What's the matter?" the bunny exclaimed. "Why won't you talk to me?" The Skin Horse's worn glass eyes still had the same kind expression the Little Rabbit remembered so well. Yet no matter how he prodded and pushed, the Skin Horse would not say hello or move even so much as a hair of his ragged tail. The Little Rabbit grew confused and anxious. "Don't you remember me?" he cried over and over again. But the Skin Horse only stared at him sadly.

Hoping to find a familiar face or sight, the Little Rabbit looked around the room. Suddenly, it was strange to him, like a place he had never seen before. A painted tin soldier gazed at him coldly from behind the open cupboard doors, and the jointed wooden lion at the foot of the bed gave him a haughty look, as if he were saying, "What do *you* think you are doing here?" To escape their awful stares, the Little Rabbit hopped up onto the bed.

The quilt covering the bed was new, and the Little Rabbit did not recognize any of the patches in it. It smelled differently, too, and was not nearly as soft as the old one.

Then he glimpsed something lying on the Boy's pillow. It was a toy rabbit. She was nestled against the pillow just as he had been once upon a time. The Little Rabbit hopped closer to have a better look at her.

She was quite splendid, indeed, made of white plush, with sparkling blue glass eyes. And around her neck she wore a fine blue satin ribbon that was almost the same shade as her eyes. He remembered where he'd seen her before. She was the new bunny the Boy had been given the night the Velveteen Rabbit had left this house forever.

He stared at the White Plush Rabbit, and he felt a dull aching in his chest that had never been there before. "Are you Real?" he said, tapping her gently with his paw. "Has the Boy made you Real?"

But of course the White Plush Rabbit could not answer, for she was only stuffed with sawdust.

"Can you hop about and dance like this?" the Little Rabbit asked her then. He twirled around on top of the quilt to demonstrate, and even did a real somersault. But still the White Plush Rabbit said nothing.

"So you aren't Real!" he exclaimed crossly. "You aren't Real at all!" You see, in a way he so wanted the White Plush Rabbit to move and speak to him. Then again, he knew that if she were Real, it would mean that the Boy loved her as much as he had loved the little Velveteen Rabbit, and he almost could not bear that.

The White Plush Rabbit just stared at him blankly with her blue glass eyes. Suddenly, the Little Rabbit did a mean thing. He nudged her with his nose as hard as he could until she fell off the Boy's bed and landed with a thump on the floor!

The instant he'd done it, he felt horribly wicked. He peered down at her from the edge of the bed. For a moment he had the odd impression that something stirred in her blue glass eyes—a glint, like a tear. And he was just about to tell her that he was sorry and he didn't know what had come over him, when he heard a very loud voice: "I don't believe it! There's a wild rabbit in here!"

It was Nana, who had always ruled the nursery, and with a very firm hand, indeed.

She had come to pull back the Boy's covers and get everything ready for bedtime, and she was quite surprised to see the Little Rabbit sitting there on the quilt. Quick as anything, Cook came dashing up the stairs, brandishing a broom. The Little Rabbit dove under the bed and peered out anxiously to see what Cook and Nana would do next.

Just then he heard the Boy's voice. "Where's the bunny rabbit?" the Boy called up the stairs.

"It was sitting right on your bed!" Nana replied. "We've got to find him and chase him out!"

The Little Rabbit wasn't sure what that meant, but Nana sounded very stern, indeed. And he was about to run for the door when he heard the Boy's footsteps come pounding up the stairs, and all at once, there he was, standing in the doorway!

The Little Rabbit poked all of his head out from under the dust ruffle. He was hoping the Boy would notice him under the bed and tell Nana and Cook to let him be. "He's my old toy Bunny I lost so long ago," he wanted the Boy to say. Nana and Cook would go away then, and he and the Boy could play just as they used to.

But the Little Rabbit saw that the Boy was not looking for him. Instead, the Boy was staring at his pillow with a puzzled expression. "Where's my Bunny?" he said. "She was right here when I went down for supper. Where is she? I have to find her!"

"I think she fell on the floor," Nana said over her shoulder, for she was busy shaking the broom in all the corners. The Boy knelt down and looked around until he spotted the White Plush Rabbit half-hidden under the bed.

"There you are!" he exclaimed happily. "How are you, my old Bunny?" He picked up the White Plush Rabbit and hugged her tight, just as he used to do with the Velveteen Rabbit. Then he whispered something in her ear. How the Little Rabbit longed to know what the Boy was saying! Was it perhaps a story about exploring the great wild at the back of the garden? Or maybe it was about visiting the seaside where he had never gotten to go and play in the waves?

The Little Rabbit had no time to think about any of that, for just then Nana spotted his head peeking out from under the bed.

"There he is!" she shrieked and came rushing at him with Cook's broom. Now he had to run as fast as he could to get away. He hopped down the steps, with Nana so close behind he could feel the broom straws whisk his tail. He was going so fast he skidded across the polished hallway floor before leaping out the window into the garden.

In the darkness of the hedge, he stopped to catch his breath and look back at the Boy's house in the moonlight. He remembered what the Skin Horse had told him in the nursery about being Real. "Once you are Real," his wise old friend had said, "you can't be a toy again. Real lasts for always." The Little Rabbit shook himself as hard as he could so as not to cry. He didn't belong to the Boy anymore, and the Boy had a new toy Bunny. He turned and started back to the woods. He did not look back either, for now he knew he was a Real wild rabbit.

Spring passed, then summer. The Little Rabbit no longer hopped to the edge of the woods and stared across the fields at the Boy's house all lit up in the darkness. Sometimes he still dreamt of those times though, and he dreamt, too, of the White Plush Rabbit and wondered if she had become Real because the Boy loved her.

Fall came with cool winds and hard rains, and soon it was winter again. The wild rabbits crept out into the fields

and dug up old potatoes and carrots the
farmers had left in the fields. At night they
huddled together in their warm burrows and told
one another long stories to make the cold, dark
winter pass more quickly.

One day the Little Rabbit went
out to hunt for turnips in the
fields. Snow was falling, and
he had not been out of the
woods long when it began to
come down more and more heavily.
He hopped this way and that through the thick, damp snow.
By and by he became lost, and although he went around
and around, he could not find his way back to the woods
and his safe, warm burrow.

Then he saw a bright light shining through the swirls of
snow, and since it looked warm and welcoming, he went
toward it. As darkness fell, the snow stopped falling, and the
sky grew clear. The Little Rabbit saw then that he was in
the Boy's garden, and just beyond was the Boy's house.

He hopped up to the back door, thinking he might find
something to eat. He knew the other wild rabbits sometimes
came there in the winter to look for food, though he had
never come with them. Just as he was nearing the house, the
door suddenly flew open. He scurried behind the coal bin as
out came Nana shivering without her coat and scarf. The
gardener was beside her, and he was carrying a brown
cloth sack.

"Just take that sack out behind the fowl house and put it in the rubbish," Nana said. "But make sure it's gone before the Boy gets back. You know what a fuss he'll make when he finds we've thrown away his old toys. Remember how he carried on when we tossed out that old velveteen rabbit of his when he had scarlet fever? Anyway, he's getting big now, and he doesn't need to play with all these toys anymore. They just lay around the nursery, and I can't tell you what a job it is tidying them all away."

As the Little Rabbit watched, the gardener slung the sack over his shoulder and carried it out to the back of the garden. But neither the gardener nor Nana noticed the little brown rabbit who peeped out at them from behind the coal bin.

When the gardener had gone and Nana had shut off the kitchen light and gone creaking up the staircase, the Little Rabbit cautiously crept out into the garden. He hopped through the snow, past the tall raspberry thickets, and across the flower beds to the fowl house.

There was the brown cloth sack. It lumped and bulged all over, just like the sack he had been put in the night the White Plush Rabbit had first come to the nursery. He sat up on his hind legs and peered into the mouth of the sack. It was very dark in there, but he thought he glimpsed a blue glass eye gleaming in the moonlight. He put his paw in the opening and nudged and tugged and wiggled the sack until it fell over. Out tumbled a toy train, some blocks, and the White Plush Rabbit.

She no longer looked nearly so grand. Her plush coat was as worn as the Velveteen Rabbit's had become. It was no longer pure white either, but stained here and there with dirt from the garden where the Boy had pushed her through burrows he had made, and with jam and chocolate that Nana had tried unsuccessfully to wash off. The pink of her ears was gray now, and her nose was quite rubbed away. The blue satin ribbon around her neck was gone, and her blue glass eyes were scratched and no longer sparkled as brightly as they once had. Yet to the Little Rabbit her expression seemed very beautiful and wise, and he thought that she looked much more splendid now than she had when she was new.

He stared at her and thought of how she, too, had been sent out from the nursery and away from the Boy who loved her. A great sadness for her came over him. He moved closer to her and nuzzled her with his nose, worried that she would be cold and afraid, lying in the wet snow.

At that very moment a silver light, like a drop from the moon, fell on the ground before him. And the Little Rabbit smelled violets and roses and lilies all around, even though it was winter and all the flowers were asleep beneath the ground. Then a voice above him said, "Don't you recognize me, Little Rabbit?"

He looked up and saw a lovely pale face smiling down at him—a smile so tender it made him sigh. It was the nursery magic Fairy! The Little Rabbit recognized her at once, but she looked so beautiful and grand that at first he could not get out a single word.

"Is it really You?" he cried at last.

"Yes, it is me," the Fairy replied. "And I have come to ask you a very great favor. Do you remember the night I made you Real?"

The Little Rabbit nodded, and he thought of that night, and of many other times, too. He remembered when he had first gone to live in the forest and how the other wild rabbits had teased him. He remembered all the times he had hopped to the edge of the fields and looked out at the Boy's house. But most of all he remembered the night when he had gone to the Boy's house and found the White Plush Rabbit lying on the Boy's pillow.

"Yes," he whispered, "I remember." And before he could help himself a tear rolled from his eye, and another, and another, until his little pink nose was quite damp.

"It is hard sometimes to be Real, isn't it?" said the Fairy kindly.

"The Skin Horse told me that sometimes it hurts to be Real," the Little Rabbit said. "He was always truthful."

"Yes," the Fairy said, "there are many wonderful things about being Real, but it can also be difficult and lonely. And I know you have often missed your old home and the Boy and all the games you two used to play together. That is why I want you to do something for me, and perhaps for yourself as well. This little white rabbit was a toy, and just like you she was Real to the Boy because he loved her. But now the Boy has no need of her. So I want you to teach her how to be truly Real—as Real as you are. Will you do that for me, Little Rabbit?"

The Little Rabbit swallowed and nodded. The Fairy's smile grew even more tender, and she leaned over and kissed his wet nose. "I knew you would," she said softly, and before he even had time to say goodbye, she was gone.

"Why did she leave so quickly?" the Little Rabbit thought. "It isn't fair! I so wanted to talk to her about being Real!" But just then he felt something strange happening near him. And looking around, he saw the White Plush Rabbit, only she was no longer a toy, but as Real as he was! The Little Rabbit was so happy then he was almost afraid he would burst for joy. He stared at the White Plush Rabbit, and she stared at him. Her eyes were blue and sparkling, and they gazed into his shyly. Then her nose twitched as she sniffed the fresh night air for the very first time. Suddenly she hopped closer to him, and it so startled her to move that she stopped. She sat up on her hind legs, a little awkwardly because she wasn't quite used to them yet.

"Hello!" she said. "Are you Real, too?"

A few minutes later, Nana looked out her window as she was turning out her light to go to sleep. "Oh, my," she said, "whatever are those two rabbits doing, leaping around the garden like that?" She decided she would have to have a word with the gardener because it was no good to have wild rabbits around, eating the flowers and vegetables. Maybe she would have to ask him to lay out some traps.

But when she mentioned it to the gardener on the following day, he only laughed. "What's the harm?" he said. "Let the little bunnies be."

"What bunnies?" said the Boy, who had just run out from the kitchen.

"Never you mind," said Nana, but the Boy made the gardener tell him about them anyway.

"How I should like to have seen them!" the Boy exclaimed. "They are just like my old toy bunnies. One brown with spots and one white. Maybe they really are mine and now they're real and they've come back to see me and make sure I miss them."

"What nonsense!" Nana sniffed, more sharply than she meant to, for she felt rather guilty about having gotten rid of all the Boy's old toys. "How can toy rabbits become real?"

But later that spring Nana could not help remembering what the Boy had said when the gardener told her about a strange thing that had happened. Early in the morning, the gardener said, he had seen two rabbits, one white and one brown with spots, and three baby rabbits with them, all sitting under the hedge in a row and peering up at the Boy's window, just as if they'd come to say hello.